Dedicated to our publisher, Tom Peterson,

who hates to read.

Designed by Rita Marshall

Text copyright © 2013 by Rita Marshall

Illustrations copyright © 2013 by Etienne Delessert

Previous ISBN 1-56846-005-5   Previous LC Control No. 92-2693

This new edition published in 2013 by Creative Editions

P.O. Box 227, Mankato, MN 56002 USA   www.thecreativecompany.us

Creative Editions is an imprint of The Creative Company

Printed in China

Library of Congress Cataloging-in-Publication Data

Marshall, Rita. I hate to read! / by Rita Marshall; illustrated by Etienne Delessert.

Summary: Victor Dickens hates to read—or so he tells his parents and teacher.

But when he's alone one night, Victor discovers that words on a page

can take him on unexpected adventures.

ISBN 978-1-56846-232-5

[1. Books and reading—Fiction. 2. Characters in literature—Fiction.]

I. Delessert, Etienne, ill. II. Title.

PZ7.M356738Iah 2013   [E]—dc23   2012014312

2 4 6 8 9 7 5 3 1

Story by Rita Marshall
Illustrations by Etienne Delessert

Creative Editions

Victor Dickens was a good kid.

He took a helmet
with him when he
skateboarded.

He combed his hair for class pictures.

He always shared with his dog, Page.

Yes, Victor Dickens was a good kid.
But Victor hated to read. He taught
Page to chew up books.

Victor got As in math and Bs in science.
But he got Fs in the ABCs. His mother
even fed him alphabet soup for lunch, but
nothing seemed to help.

One evening, Victor was pretending to read so he could watch TV. A crocodile in a white coat crawled out of the book. "Jump into my pocket, if you like to read," the crocodile said. "It's story time."

"I hate to read!" Victor said.

Then a little mouse chewed her way out of the book. "You'll find gold in this book!" she cried. "Plant the coins—you'll get rich with ideas!"

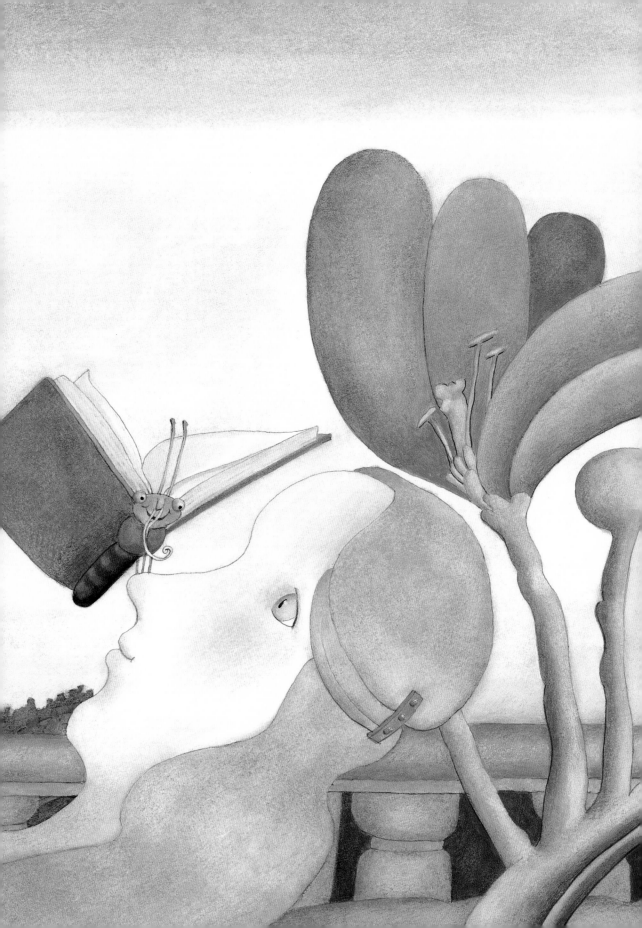

Victor turned the page. The Beauty
looked like Natalie Nickerson. And

Natalie had just invited him to her birthday
party. How embarrassing! Victor slammed
the book shut.

It was almost dark when a strange bird appeared at the window with a glowworm in her beak. "It's fun to read, Victor Dickens," she whispered. "Especially when you're not supposed to!"

By now, Victor was missing his favorite TV
show. But the strange thing was that Victor didn't
mind. He closed his eyes—and imagined Page
as a book-eating monster.

Then he imagined his teacher with a black hat. She was throwing books into a boiling pot. "We hate to read!" his classmates at Salisbury Central School were chanting. Natalie Nickerson was the loudest.

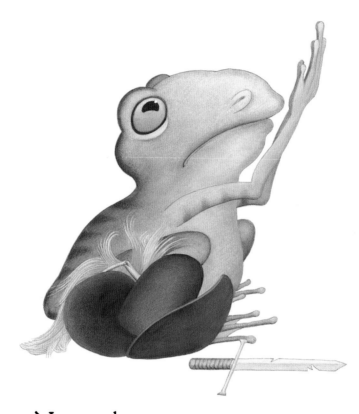

Nervously, Victor turned another page.
Out popped a slippery frog with a tiny
sword. "Read the page so I can turn into a
prince!" he croaked. "Then I'll kiss the
Sleeping Beauty and wake her up."

The rabbit didn't wait for Victor to finish.
He leaped over the house and called back,
"You're missing the boo-o-oot!"

"Come along, boy, we'll cross the ocean," the rabbit said. "It'll be a story for *The New York Times*!"

"But I hate stories," answered Victor. "And I hate to …"

A rabbit in black boots suddenly jumped
out of the parrot's hat. He winked at Victor.

When a parrot with a peg leg hobbled into
the room, Victor wondered if he was dream-
ing. The parrot pulled out a treasure map.
"Fly with me to the Spice Islands!"

"Never!" Victor huffed. "I hate adventures!"

"Go step on a mousetrap!"

Victor snapped. "I hate books!"

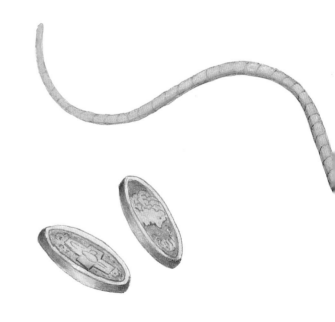

Instead of joining in, Victor opened
his eyes. What were the crocodile, mouse,
parrot, rabbit, frog, and strange bird up
to now? Victor picked up the book.

"We hate to read! We hate to read!" The
chant continued. But Victor opened the
book to look for his new friends. As he
read each page, he just hated … to come
to the end.